LITTLE HOUSE · Laura Ingalls Wilder

MY FIRST LITTLE HOUSE BOOKS

WINTER DAYS ❧ IN THE BIG WOODS

ADAPTED FROM THE LITTLE HOUSE BOOKS

By Laura Ingalls Wilder

Illustrated by Renée Graef

SCHOLASTIC INC.
New York Toronto London Auckland Sydney

For Tim
—R.G.

ISBN 0-590-25219-4

Text copyright © 1932 by Laura Ingalls Wilder.
Copyright renewed © 1959, 1987 by Roger L. MacBride.
Illustrations copyright © 1994 by Renée Graef.
All rights reserved. Published by Scholastic Inc., 555 Broadway, New York, NY 10012, by arrangement with HarperCollins Publishers, Inc.

12 11 10 9 8 7 6 5 4 3 2 1   5 6 7 8 9/9 0/0

Printed in the U.S.A.

First Scholastic printing, January 1995

Illustrations for the My First Little House Books are inspired by the work of Garth Williams with his permission, which we gratefully acknowledge.

Once upon a time, a little girl named Laura lived in the Big Woods of Wisconsin in a little house made of logs.

Laura lived in the little house with her Pa, her Ma, her big sister Mary, her baby sister Carrie, and their good old bulldog Jack.

Winter was coming to the Big Woods. Soon the little house would be covered with snow. Pa went hunting every day so that they would have meat during the long, cold winter.

Ma, Laura, and Mary gathered potatoes and
carrots, beets and turnips, cabbages and onions,
and peppers and pumpkins from the garden next to
the little house.

By the time winter came, the little house was full of good things to eat. Laura and Mary thought the attic was a lovely place to play. They played house by using the round orange pumpkins as tables and chairs, and everything was snug and cozy.

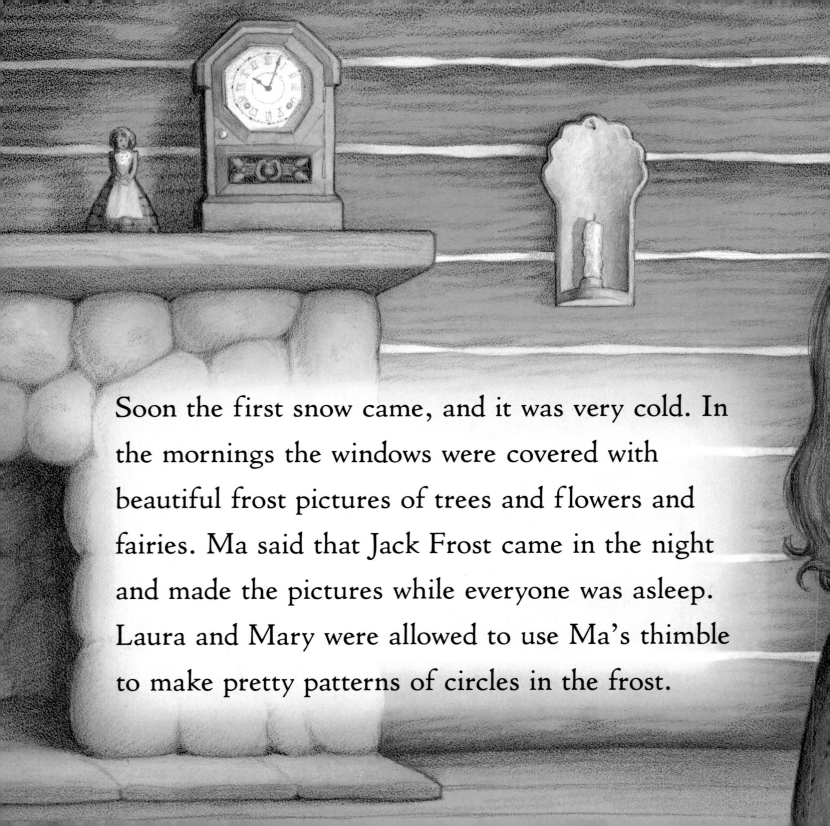

Soon the first snow came, and it was very cold. In the mornings the windows were covered with beautiful frost pictures of trees and flowers and fairies. Ma said that Jack Frost came in the night and made the pictures while everyone was asleep. Laura and Mary were allowed to use Ma's thimble to make pretty patterns of circles in the frost.

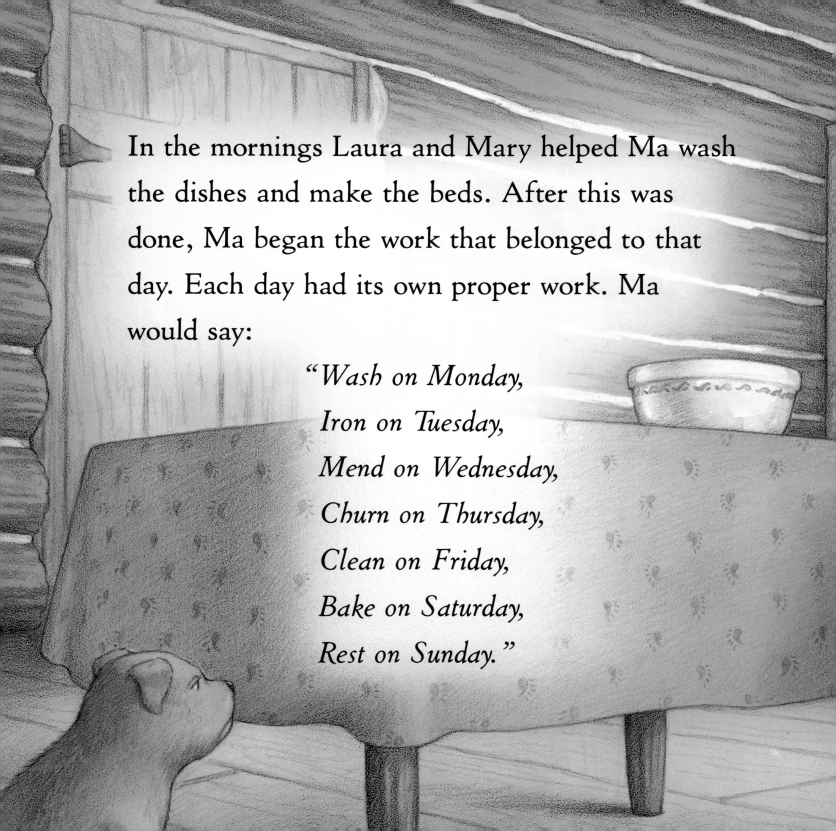

In the mornings Laura and Mary helped Ma wash the dishes and make the beds. After this was done, Ma began the work that belonged to that day. Each day had its own proper work. Ma would say:

"Wash on Monday,
Iron on Tuesday,
Mend on Wednesday,
Churn on Thursday,
Clean on Friday,
Bake on Saturday,
Rest on Sunday."

Laura liked the churning and baking days best of all. Ma had to churn the cream for a long time until it turned into butter. Mary could sometimes churn while Ma rested, but Laura was too little.

On Saturdays, when Ma made the bread, Laura
and Mary each had a little piece of dough to make

into a little loaf. Ma even gave them a bit of
cookie dough to make little cookies.

After the day's work was done, Ma would sometimes cut out paper dolls for Laura and Mary. She
drew their faces on with a pencil, and cut dresses,
hats, and ribbons out of colored paper so that
Mary and Laura could dress their dolls beautifully.

But the best time of all was at night, when Pa came home. He would throw off his fur cap and coat and mittens and call, "Where's my little half-pint of sweet cider half drunk up?" That was Laura, because she was so small.

Sometimes Pa would take down his fiddle and sing. Pa would keep time with his foot. Laura and Mary would clap their hands to the music when he sang:

"*Yankee Doodle went to town,*
He wore his striped trousies,
He swore he couldn't see the town,
There was so many houses."

Other times Pa would tell stories. When Laura and Mary begged him for a story, he would take them on his knees and tickle their faces with his long whiskers until they laughed out loud. His eyes were blue and merry.

Outside it was cold and snowy, but the little log cabin was snug and cozy. Pa, Ma, Laura, Mary,

and Baby Carrie were comfortable and happy in their little house in the Big Woods.